Chicken Licken

A Red Fox Book

Published by Random House Children's Books
20 Vauxhall Bridge Road, London SW1V 2SA

A division of The Random House Group Ltd
London Melbourne Sydney Auckland
Johannesburg and agencies throughout the world

3 5 7 9 10 8 6 4 2

First published in Great Britain by Andersen Press Ltd 1998
Red Fox edition 2000

Printed in Hong Kong

THE RANDOM HOUSE GROUP Limited Reg. No. 954009
www.randomhouse.co.uk

ISBN 0-09-940446-X

Chicken Licken

Michael Foreman

RED FOX

Chicken Licken was scratching for worms,
when an acorn fell on his head.
He got such a fright that half his feathers fell out.
"Help! Help!" he cried. "The sky is falling!
I must go and tell the King!"
And off he ran.

On his way, he met Henny Penny.
"Where are you going in such a hurry?"
she clucked.
"The sky is falling and I'm on my way
to tell the King!" said Chicken Licken.

"I'll come with you,"
said Henny Penny,

and on they ran.

By and by, they met Ducky Lucky.
"Where are you going in such a hurry?"
he quacked.
"The sky is falling and we're on our way
to tell the King!" said Henny Penny.

"I'll come with you,"
said Ducky Lucky,

and on they ran.

Sooner than later, they met Goosey Loosey.
"Where are you going in such a hurry?"
she honked.
"The sky is falling and we're on our way
to tell the King!" said Ducky Lucky.

"I'll come with you,"
said Goosey Loosey,

and on they ran . . .

. . . pell mell into Turkey Lurkey.
"Where are you going in such a hurry?"
he gobbled.
"The sky is falling, and we're on our way
to tell the King!" said Goosey Loosey.

"I'll come with you,"
said Turkey Lurkey,

and on they ran.

At the edge of the wood, they met Foxy Loxy.
"Wherever are you going in such a hurry?"
asked Foxy Loxy.
"The sky is falling," they chorused all five,
"and we're on our way to tell the King!"

"Are you, indeed?" said Foxy Loxy.
"Allow me to show you the way."

So Chicken Licken, Henny Penny,
Ducky Lucky, Goosey Loosey and
Turkey Lurkey followed Foxy Loxy,

who had no intention of taking
them to the King.
He led them straight to his lair . . .

and what happened there gave them
such a fright that ALL their feathers fell out
and they quite forgot that the sky was falling in.
So they never did get to tell the King.

And Chicken Licken? The last *I* heard—

he was running still . . .

Phew!

Some bestselling Red Fox picture books

THE BIG ALFIE AND ANNIE ROSE STORYBOOK
by Shirley Hughes
OLD BEAR
by Jane Hissey
OI! GET OFF OUR TRAIN
by John Burningham
DON'T DO THAT!
by Tony Ross
NOT NOW, BERNARD
by David McKee
ALL JOIN IN
by Quentin Blake
THE WHALES' SONG
by Gary Blythe and Dyan Sheldon
JESUS' CHRISTMAS PARTY
by Nicholas Allan
THE PATCHWORK CAT
by Nicola Bayley and William Mayne
WILLY AND HUGH
by Anthony Browne
THE WINTER HEDGEHOG
by Ann and Reg Cartwright
A DARK, DARK TALE
by Ruth Brown
HARRY, THE DIRTY DOG
by Gene Zion and Margaret Bloy Graham
DR XARGLE'S BOOK OF EARTHLETS
by Jeanne Willis and Tony Ross
WHERE'S THE BABY?
by Pat Hutchins